LETTERS
BY THE
CREEK

LETTERS
*C*REEK
BY THE

BY

JULIE HART

ILLUSTRATIONS BY
JUSTIN BRANCH

Dove
Publishers

Bladensburg, MD

Letters by the Creek
Published by
Inscript Books
a division of Dove Christian Publishers
P.O. Box 611
Bladensburg, MD 20710-0611
www.dovechristianpublishers.com

Cover Design by Raenita Wiggins

Cover and interior illustrations by Justin Branch

Photographs by Jordan Hart

ISBN: 978-1-7359529-1-8

Library of Congress Catalog No. 2020949976

Published in the United States of America
25 24 23 22 21 20 1 2 3 4 5

To my mother, Jewel Dean Elledge Cook. Although you are no longer with me on this Earth, your inspiration, encouraging words and stories will remain with me forever.

To everyone who feels discouraged and hopeless about something in your life, remember the words from the Book of Matthew written many years ago but still true today:
"With God, All Things are Possible."

1

Best Friends Forever

*T*he giant yellow school bus screeched to a halt, letting two giggly little girls off at the end of the dusty dirt road. They still had a long walk ahead of them before reaching their houses at the end of the road, but they didn't mind. When they were together, it didn't matter what they were doing. Whether it was walking home, doing homework, or anything else, they had fun. Especially on days like today, the last day of school. Summer vacation had finally arrived. They had so many plans for the summer, and all of them included each other.

One of those little girls was Jewel Dean Elledge. She lived at the end of that dirt road in a small house nestled at the edge of a creek in a place called Blackburn's Hollow, in North Carolina, named after her mother's side of the family. Surrounding her house were mountains that had been traveled by the famous explorer, Daniel Boone, many years ago. Jewel lived with her mom and dad, two older brothers, and two younger sisters.

Being the middle child was hard sometimes. There was always work to be done. Jewel's family didn't have a lot of money. They had no running water, no inside bathroom, and with five hungry children to be fed, there wasn't always a lot of food. With WWII raging, money was especially scarce.

Often, Jewel would have to babysit her younger sisters while her mom worked in the garden or cooked for the family. She would also help her mom with household chores. Sometimes she would even help her dad in his garage. She would fetch tools for him or sweep up the messes that he made while he worked on cars that belonged to other people. Jewel had many grown-up responsibilities, but when all her chores were done and her schoolwork was complete, she would spend her free time with her best friend, Claudine.

Claudine lived on the other side of the creek in a much larger home. Her house had an upstairs and a downstairs, a large kitchen, and the greatest thing around that no one else in Blackburn's Hollow had: running water from a fresh spring. She didn't have to go outside and fetch a bucket of water just to have a drink. She didn't have to push and pull a pump like everyone else did. Claudine's family didn't have to store their food outside in the nearby spring in order to keep it from spoiling either. They had the luxury of cold spring water right in their kitchen.

Jewel loved going to Claudine's house. She loved all the luxuries that Claudine had, but most of all, Jewel loved playing with Claudine, and Claudine loved playing with Jewel. They enjoyed all the same things, and they liked doing them together. They loved running barefoot in the fields in front of their houses. They loved splashing in the creek that separated their homes, catching crawdads, fish, and other creatures. On hot summer days, they enjoyed cooling off with a swim in the creek. They also loved climbing the tall mountains behind their houses, pretending to be like Daniel Boone when he explored the trails leading to the Blue Ridge Parkway. Jewel and Claudine would always find something to do together, even if it was just walking and talking down the long, dusty road that led to their houses.

As they played, they talked about what they wanted to be when they grew up. They daydreamed about who they would marry and what they would name their children. Yes, this was all just daydreaming, as twelve-year-old girls often do, but one thing was for sure: they knew that no matter what happened when they grew up, they would remain best friends.

Often, they would confirm their friendship by picking a small purplish-blue flower that grew down by the creek. The girls knew these flowers were called forget-me-nots, so sometimes they ended their playdates by handing each other a freshly picked forget-me-not, along with a pinkie promise to remain best friends forever.

2

Polio hits close to Home

*N*ot long after school let out for the summer, Jewel overheard her mother talking to her older brothers, Bruce and Bryan. Somewhere in the conversation, she heard her mother talking about someone in the community with a sick baby boy.

"Mama, what's wrong with Baby Charles?" Jewel asked.

"He has poliovirus and is in the hospital in Hickory," her mother replied.

"What's poliovirus?" Jewel asked.

"It's a bad virus that can cause people to lose their ability to walk and sometimes makes breathing difficult. Many people who have polio don't get better, and if they live, they might be in a wheelchair or leg braces for the rest of their life. Baby Charles is getting help from the doctors and nurses in Hickory."

"Will he be OK?" Jewel asked.

Her mother tried to look positive. "We're hoping and praying for the best."

This worried Jewel because she didn't like to think about anybody being sick, especially a baby. Jewel told Claudine, and they decided they would make some cards to give to Baby Charles's family. Jewel and Claudine's mothers wouldn't allow their girls to deliver the cards to the family and told them they could send the cards through the mail. Jewel and Claudine didn't quite understand why they weren't allowed to go there, but they obeyed their parents.

Soon Jewel was hearing about more and more people who had polio. Most were being sent to hospitals nearby, with the greatest number going to the hospital in Hickory. It was an emergency hospital about an hour away that had been set up to help people with polio. Many of the people who had polio lived nearby, and most were children or babies.

Sometimes Jewel heard her mom and dad talking in low voices about all the new cases that they had read about in the local newspaper. Not liking to hear about this terrible virus, which seemed to be striking more and more people, Jewel would cup her hands over her ears and run outside to keep from worrying more than she already did.

3

SAD NEWS

$\mathcal{N}$ot too far into the summer, Jewel and Claudine heard some devastating news. Because of the polio epidemic, which seemed to be hitting the entire community, the health department encouraged parents to keep their children away from other children. Since there was no vaccine or cure for this mysterious illness, parents, including Jewel and Claudine's, were frightened by it and followed the health department's guidelines. This meant Jewel and Claudine couldn't play together for a while, at least until the polio epidemic was over. No more walks down the long, dusty road together. No more pretending to be explorers. No more running through the fields or splashing in the creek. Jewel and Claudine were very sad, but they obeyed their parents.

One day, Jewel was outside her house helping her mom pick corn from the garden. As she stretched to reach an ear of corn from a tall stalk, she spotted Claudine playing outside with her sisters. They were heading for the creek. Oh, how Jewel wanted to run down to the creek to see her! She missed her friend so much and wanted to splash barefoot in the creek with her or sit on the creek bank and have a conversation with her, but she knew she wasn't allowed, at least not yet. The polio epidemic was far from over. In fact, little did they know, but it was only just getting started.

Knowing the answer before she asked but deciding to ask anyway, Jewel pleaded with her mom. "Mama, may I go down to the creek and see Claudine? No one in her family has polio, and no one in our family has it, so why can't we play together?"

Jewel's mom wrapped her arms around her daughter. "No one has polio that we *know of,* but we have to play it safe for a little while longer," she said gently. "Hopefully, by the end of summer, the polio epidemic will be over, and you can play with Claudine again. I know you miss her, and I'm sorry."

With tears in her eyes, Jewel nodded and simply waved at Claudine from a distance.

4

AN IDEA

$\mathcal{A}$s the days went by, Jewel and Claudine missed each other more and more. They knew that staying apart was for their own safety, but they just *had* to think of a way to talk. Neither of them had a telephone, so they thought about mailing letters to each other. Still, even though stamps cost just three cents, it was too expensive for Jewel to mail a letter very often. She had no money of her own, and she couldn't ask her parents. It took every penny they had to keep their household running.

Feeling discouraged, Jewel went to talk to her mom for comfort, as she always did. She found her standing over a big pot of boiling water. She was canning some fresh vegetables to put away for the winter months.

"Mama, I miss Claudine so much. I have so much to tell her, and I wish I could just meet her at the creek to talk for a bit," Jewel said.

"I know you miss her," Mama replied in her soft but firm voice, "and this epidemic will eventually pass, but you can't risk getting polio and passing it along to the family. We certainly can't afford any medicine if we do get the virus, and Honey, it's a very scary virus. It can leave you crippled for the rest of your life. This virus seems to attack children more often, and I don't want you or any of your brothers or sisters taking a chance at catching it. Why don't you write Claudine a letter? You both know how to read and write, so there's no reason why you can't."

"I thought about writing a letter, but I don't have any money for a stamp, and I didn't want to ask you and Daddy because I know that money is tight."

Jewel's mother smiled at her with loving eyes. "Use your imagination and creativity, Jewel. You two girls are always inventing things and finding ways to overcome obstacles that come your way."

Jewel thought and thought as she watched her mother seal the Mason jar after putting freshly snapped and boiled green beans into it. Then she got a brilliant idea. "Mama, do you think you have enough jars for me to have one?"

"What on Earth are you going to do with a Mason jar?" her mother asked as she sealed another jar.

"You'll see!" Jewel exclaimed. So, her mother took a jar from her collection, and with a smile on her face, she gently placed it in Jewel's outstretched hand.

5
THE MAILBOX BY THE CREEK

*C*lasping the jar tightly, Jewel ran as fast as her legs would carry her to the woodshed. In the back corner of the shed, she had an old milk crate with a collection of art supplies that her teachers had given her at the end of each school year. She took some scrap paper and crayons and drew a picture, just large enough to cover her Mason jar. She drew a picture of two girls, one on each side. One girl had light-brown hair like Jewel, and the other had dark-brown hair like Claudine. She included the number 74 on it because seven was her favorite number and four was Claudine's. Using some glue that she created using flour and water, she wrapped the picture around the Mason jar. She even drew and cut out a red flag, attaching it to the jar's lid. When her mailbox was finished, she ran to the creek to find a safe, secure place to put it.

When she reached the edge of the creek, she saw the little bridge that she and Claudine had used so often to cross over to each other's field. Hanging over the center of the bridge was a low tree branch that she would sometimes swing from while crossing the bridge. Where the branch attached to the sturdy trunk of the old River Oak tree would be the perfect place to secure the mailbox. She carefully pushed the jar in the nook where the branch and the trunk met and then ran as quickly as she could back to the house to write her first letter to her greatly missed friend.

6

THE FIRST LETTER

$\mathcal{J}$ewel looked for a quiet corner in her house, so she could write her first letter to her long-lost playmate. She had so much to say to Claudine, but finding a quiet place amid a large family and a small house was more difficult than Jewel imagined. She spotted the ladder that pulled down from the ceiling, leading up to the attic. Jewel had hoped that one day her daddy could make the attic her bedroom, so she wouldn't have to share a room with her younger sisters. It could be a place where she could invite Claudine to spend the night. For now, it would be a perfect place to get away and write her letter. On a sunny day like today, there would be just enough sunlight coming through the attic windows for Jewel to see.

Carefully, she climbed the ladder, taking a blanket and pillow to rest on, along with her pen and paper from her leftover school supplies. Jewel sat for a few minutes to collect her thoughts, and then she began her first letter to Claudine.

Dear Claudine,
I have so much to say to you that I don't even know where to begin. I miss you more than you know. I miss our walks down the road. I miss climbing the big hill behind your house. I miss climbing

the old apple tree to reach the highest and juiciest apples. I miss blowing dandelions and watching them fly through the air, wondering where they'll land. I miss all the secrets we used to tell each other and making pinkie promises not to tell anybody else. I miss spending the night at your house. I can't wait to see you again, but until then, maybe we can keep in touch with this mailbox I made. We can write letters to each other and put them in this jar, and it won't even cost any money to mail it. Please write back as soon as you can. I can't wait to read a letter from you.

Love,
Jewel

Jewel folded her letter and then climbed down the attic ladder. She ran as fast as she could to the creek. She crossed the wobbly boards of the bridge until she reached the branch that held the mailbox. She unscrewed the jar's lid, placing her folded letter inside. She carefully screwed the lid back on, making sure it was tight. She didn't want her letter to fall out or get wet in case it rained. Then she returned the jar to its place. Now all she could do was hope that Claudine saw the mailbox and found the letter because she had no way of telling her it was there.

7

FINALLY FOUND

*U*nfortunately, the weather wasn't very cooperative for the next few days. It rained, and the wind blew for what seemed like an eternity. Jewel had hoped her letter would have been found by now, but the stormy weather kept everyone from going outside.

Day and night, it rained. Jewel would sit at the kitchen window of her tiny house and watch the creek rise higher and higher. She also watched the branch holding her makeshift mailbox sway back and forth.

One day, as she was watching, she saw something fall from the tree. Could it be the jar holding her letter to her friend before she even had a chance to read it? This was more than Jewel could bear. Tears streamed down her face. Jewel's mother lovingly laid a gentle hand upon her daughter's shoulders. "Don't worry," she whispered. "It won't rain forever." Jewel wasn't so sure. She had finally come up with a plan to communicate with Claudine, and now she wasn't sure if Claudine would even get her letter.

Finally, one morning as Jewel lay in her bed, she was awakened by a bright light shining in her eyes. It was coming through her window. Could it really be sunlight? Jewel leaped from her bed onto the bare wood floor and raced outside. For a moment, she had forgotten that she was still wearing her nightgown, but she didn't care.

Her father was across the dirt road at his garage. When he saw Jewel, he yelled for her to go back inside and get dressed, so she did. After putting on her clothes, she raced back outside to check her mailbox. Sure enough, the wind and rain had destroyed the paper label and flag she had worked so hard on, but thankfully, it hadn't destroyed her letter. It was safe and secure inside the jar that was still nestled in the corner of the tree. Just as she was turning to make her way back across the bridge, she saw Claudine coming out onto the front porch of her house. Jewel waved her arms and pointed to the place that held her letter to Claudine. Then she turned and headed back to her house, watching and waiting to see if her friend understood what she was trying to tell her. Jewel's mother called her inside to eat breakfast. Right as she was approaching the back door of her house, she saw Claudine making her way down to the creek!

8

A Letter in Return

$\mathcal{J}$ewel couldn't eat her breakfast fast enough! After practically swallowing her last bite whole, she jumped up from the table to run back outside. Before she made it to the door, she was stopped by her father, who told her to stay seated at the table until everyone was finished eating. She helped her mother feed her little sister, Carol. After everyone had finally taken their last bites, Jewel helped her mother clear the table and wash and dry the dishes. When the last dish had been put away, Jewel's mother asked her to watch her younger sisters while she did some housework.

Jewel threw Carol on her hip and grabbed Martha by the hand. Then she raced down to the creek, practically dragging Martha along behind her. She sat her sisters in the grass on the bank of the creek, forbidding them to move while she went to check her mailbox. The letter was gone! Claudine had retrieved her letter from the jar! At least Jewel hoped it was her friend who had taken it and not someone else.

After playing jump rope and hopscotch with her sisters, she took them to the front porch in the old glider and read them a story. While reading, she glanced toward Claudine's house and saw her friend race outside, the screen door slamming behind her. Claudine jumped off her big wrap-around porch and made her way down to the creek once again. Jewel noticed she was carrying something. Could it be a letter for her?

Claudine skipped to the bridge and reached for the jar. Yes, Jewel was sure it was a letter for her as she saw Claudine screw the lid back onto the jar after placing something inside. After giving Claudine time to get back away from the creek, Jewel dragged her sisters back down the bank to get her long-awaited letter. Here is what it said.

Dear Jewel,

I miss all the things you miss and more! I miss playing house in the old barn with our dolls. I miss pretending to be explorers as we hike up the mountain. I wish we could just wade in the creek together and pick forget-me-nots. Mama doesn't know when we'll be able to play together again, but I hope it's soon. It's boring without you. We can't even go to church anymore. I'm glad you thought of a way for us to write letters to each other. This was a great idea you had for a mailbox. I can't wait to get the next letter from you. I left a gift for you along with this letter. Hold onto it, and re-member you are my best friend and always will be.

Love,
Claudine

Along with the letter, Jewel found something wrapped in tissue paper. It was a beautiful necklace that she had always admired, which belonged to Claudine. It was a gold chain with a small heart-shaped locket. Jewel opened the locket, and inside it had a tiny picture of Claudine on one side, and on the other side, it said, *"BFF."* Jewel knew that this meant, "Best Friends Forever."

9

BAD NEWS

$\mathcal{F}$or the next few days, Jewel and Claudine wrote letters to each other every day. They found more and more things to write about and would often leave small gifts for each other. Most of the gifts Jewel left for Claudine were homemade.

One afternoon, Jewel went to the mailbox by the creek, hoping to find a letter from Claudine. Jewel had written the last letter, and it was time for Claudine to put a return letter in the mailbox for Jewel. Once again, though, the jar was empty. Jewel was confused and saddened by the sight of the empty jar. Why wasn't Claudine writing her back? Could Jewel have said something in her last letter that made Claudine angry? Did Claudine not like the gifts that Jewel had made her? Compared to the nice gifts that Claudine had given her, they weren't very valuable, but they were made from the heart. Things like that never seemed to bother Claudine before. A million thoughts and questions raced through Jewel's mind. She even went back and reread the last letter that Claudine had written to her to see if she could detect anything that had gone wrong.

Dear Jewel,
This week hasn't been the greatest. It's bad enough not being able to go to church or town, but

now Mama and Daddy say we have to play quietly in our rooms because Midge has been awful fussy and won't hardly eat anything. When she finally sleeps, we have to be extra quiet so we don't disturb her. She also started running a fever yesterday, but Mama and Daddy said they don't think it's anything but a summer bug. At least that's what we're hoping. Anyway, until next time, stay safe and well.

Your friend,
Claudine

Claudine hadn't written a long letter that last time, and there was no gift with it, but she didn't seem mad or upset with Jewel. Jewel's imagination started running wild with possibilities when suddenly she saw a man in a black suit and hat approaching the front porch of Claudine's house. Jewel watched as he stepped onto the porch and placed something on the front door. Who was this man, and what did he put on Claudine's door? It was some sort of sign, but she couldn't read it from so far away.

Once again, Jewel was confused, but this time different questions filled her mind. She just *had* to know what had been placed on her best friend's door. Was that why Claudine hadn't written her in several days? Jewel couldn't go to Claudine's house to find out what the sign said, but she knew someone who would be willing to take the risk. Someone who wasn't afraid to break the rules or disobey their parents. That someone was Jewel's older brother, Bryan. Bryan was always getting into mischief. He didn't seem to mind getting into trouble; in fact, he seemed to enjoy it. Usually, Jewel scolded Bryan for his careless actions. Still, today he seemed to be the perfect person for finding out information that she just *had* to know.

She ran back up the hill into the house in search of her brother. She raced from room to room, yelling Bryan's name until her mother shushed her. "Carol is napping, and if you wake her, you're gonna be babysitting because I have work to get done. Why the panicked search for Bryan? Usually, you try to keep your distance from his teasing and pranking."

Jewel paused for a moment, taking in her mother's words. Mama was right; Bryan was constantly teasing her and pranking her. Only a few days ago, she had placed a school picture of herself in the mailbox by the creek with a note on the back for Claudine. It said, "To Claudine, my best friend forever, Jewel Dean, age 12." But before Claudine had a chance to retrieve the picture from the mailbox, Bryan had snuck down to the creek with a chicken dropping, placing it on top of Jewel's picture and ruining it. Jewel thought that was one of the meanest and nastiest pranks that Bryan had played on her, and she cried as she told her Mama and Daddy. The spanking Bryan received from Daddy wasn't enough to make her feel better. So, Bryan definitely owed her a favor.

Not wanting to tell her mother why she needed Bryan's help, she apologized for almost waking Carol and then started for the door.

"Try looking in your daddy's garage," her mother whispered. "He and Bruce were helping him earlier today on Mr. Smith's car."

Once again, Jewel raced out the front door searching for Bryan, this time being careful not to let the screen door slam. Mama was right; Jewel spotted Bryan in the corner of the old garage wiping grease from his hands. She waited patiently for her daddy to step out behind the garage for a breath of fresh air before she approached Bryan with her plea. She told him all about what she had seen and the sign that the man had placed on Claudine's door. Bryan agreed that it sounded like a much more exciting job than continuing his work in the garage. He told Bruce to cover for him while he conducted his investigation at Claudine's house.

Just as Jewel expected, it didn't take her sly, skillful brother long to find out what the sign said, but what she didn't expect was the news he brought to her. Bryan explained as best as he could what he had read on Claudine's door. Although Bryan couldn't remember the exact words on the sign, it was enough for Jewel to believe that someone in Claudine's house had been diagnosed with polio.

10

Long Days Ahead

$\mathcal{I}$t didn't take long, even in the days before cell phones and social media, for the word to get out. Soon everybody was talking about how Claudine's baby sister, Midge, had poliomyelitis. Although no one else in the house had any symptoms, the rest of the family was quarantined to their house. This meant no one could leave or enter the house under any circumstances. Jewel knew she wouldn't be receiving any letters any time soon, but she decided she would continue writing letters to Claudine, placing them in the mailbox by the creek. She knew Claudine wouldn't be able to read her letters, but it was still important for Jewel to continue writing them, and that is exactly what she did for the next few days.

In her letters, she told Claudine that she was praying for her and her family and couldn't wait until this horrible time had passed. She wrote poems, drew pictures, and even included dried flowers with the tear-stained notes to her best friend.

When Jewel's mother noticed Jewel's discouragement, she would often remind her, "When in doubt, pray it out." So, true to her word, Jewel prayed for Claudine every night before she went to sleep. She also prayed for Midge and for Claudine's entire family. She prayed that this horrible epidemic would soon be over.

One day as she was sitting on the creek bank thinking and blowing dandelions, she saw a car pull up the long, winding driveway that led to Claudine's house. She recognized the box-shaped vehicle right away along with the bright red letters on the side. The red light on top also confirmed what she already knew. It was an ambulance.

She watched as a small stretcher carrying a tiny body rolled from the front door of the house to the back doors of the long white ambulance. The driver loaded the small figure in the back, then closed the doors. For a moment, she caught a glimpse of Claudine standing at the doorway of her house watching as her baby sister was taken away. Before the door closed, she waved halfheartedly to Jewel. She watched as the ambulance pulled away and disappeared from sight at the curve of the dirt road, leaving nothing behind but a trail of dust in the air.

Once again, Jewel's heart raced with wonder. Where were they taking Midge? Would she be OK, or had polio claimed another innocent life? She was just a baby with a whole lifetime ahead of her. If she survived, would she have to go through life crippled and dependent on a wheelchair or leg braces? Jewel had heard about some people getting treatment in something called an iron lung. It was a device that could help people after polio had caused their chest muscles to become paralyzed, which made breathing difficult. Would Midge have to be confined to an iron lung? If so, for how long? Jewel had heard of people having to stay in an iron lung for a long time. All these questions tumbled around in Jewel's mind.

Sure enough, it wasn't long before Jewel's mother told

her that Baby Midge had been taken to the hospital in Hickory. That was the same place where Baby Charles and many other polio patients had been taken. Many were indeed using an iron lung to breathe.

Jewel didn't understand how Midge could have caught the virus in the first place when no one else in their family seemed to have it. Her mother explained that sometimes people were asymptomatic, which meant they had the virus but didn't have any symptoms. That's why it was important to keep a distance between friends and neighbors until the terrible epidemic was over. The virus was very contagious, and it was spreading from person to person like wildfire. Jewel had heard more than she could stand. It was bad enough that this virus was keeping her from her best friend. Now it seemed like it was hitting too close to home. An innocent baby living on the other side of the creek was sick. A little girl who Jewel had often held and played with while visiting her friend was now in a nearby hospital, fighting for her life.

11

GOOD NEWS

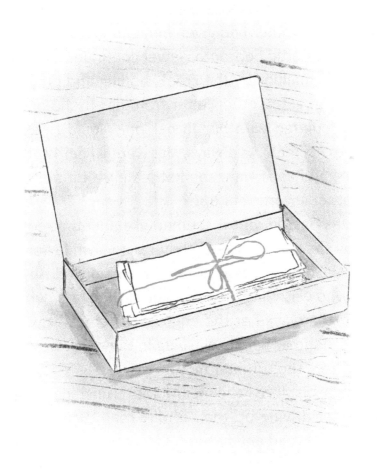

$\mathcal{D}$ay after day, Jewel continued writing letters to Claudine. Soon the little jar was full of letters, so Jewel took them out and bundled them together with an old piece of string. She placed the bundle inside an old empty cigar box her father had given her, and she put the box in her pretend attic bedroom. Jewel continued putting letters in the mailbox by the creek, hoping and praying she would soon get another letter from her friend or, better yet, be reunited with her in person. Would things ever return to normal? As always, she went to her mother for comfort, and as always, she left feeling a bit better after her mother's words of hope.

A week passed, but it seemed like a lifetime to Jewel. One day she was outside with her sisters while her mother worked in the garden. Jewel was keeping a close eye on Carol, who was lying on a blanket in the grass, while she and Martha played at the edge of the creek. It was well into the summer when splashing in the creek was a great retreat from the summer heat.

From a distance, she heard the crunching of gravel from a car driving up the old dirt road. Being near the end of a dirt road and in the midst of a polio epidemic, it was unusual to have many cars drive far enough down the road for Jewel to see. She assumed it was someone coming to get their car worked on in her daddy's garage. Jewel glanced up and then did a double-take. *Oh, no! Surely no one else in Claudine's house is sick!* Jewel thought frantically.

She leaped out of the creek and ran up the hill to take a closer look. She watched as the ambulance drove up Claudine's long, winding driveway once again. Whispering a prayer to herself, her eyes followed the driver as he went around to the back of the ambulance and opened the doors.

At that moment, the front door of Claudine's house sprang open, and out ran Claudine's entire family. Jewel celebrated from a distance along with Claudine's family at the sight that awaited them. The ambulance was bringing Baby Midge back home. She was better! In fact, Jewel learned later that she didn't actually have infantile poliomyelitis but rather a virus that mimicked polio symptoms. Regardless of what she had, God had answered their prayers of healing, and she was going to be OK.

Before leaving, the ambulance driver removed the quarantine sign that had been placed on Claudine's door.

Jewel was so excited that she ran as fast as she could to the house to tell her mom. Just as she was reaching the porch, she made a quick U-turn and raced back down to the creek bank to grab her sisters, who she had completely forgotten about! Her mother rejoiced along with Jewel as soon as she heard the news.

12
REUNITED AT LAST

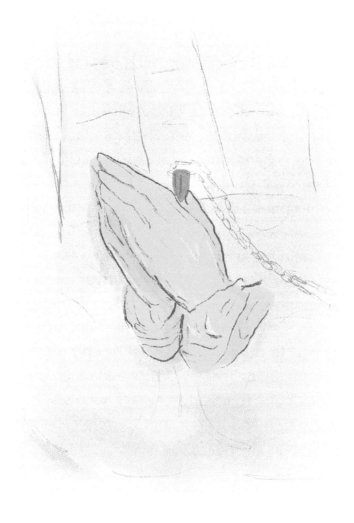

$\mathcal{I}$t wasn't long before Jewel received her long-awaited letter from Claudine.

Dear Jewel,

I'm so sorry you are just now getting this letter now. I'm sure you heard what happened to Midge, but now she's home, so we can go outside once again. We were so scared we were going to lose my baby sister. She was having trouble breathing, and when the ambulance picked her up, she was so weak she couldn't even cry. I didn't think I'd ever see her again after they took her away. Thankfully, the doctor told us yesterday that she's going to be OK. I know you were praying for her, and I thank you. We all thank you. I miss you and can't wait to see you, but for now, here's another gift to remember how your prayers really worked and to remind you that I'm still your best friend forever.

Love,
Claudine

Wrapped inside a piece of tattered tissue paper was a gold chain. Hanging from the chain was a pair of tiny hands folded in prayer. It was another one of Claudine's necklaces that Jewel had always loved. Every time the two girls played dress-up at Claudine's house, Jewel chose this necklace to wear. She adored the way the hands were folded as if in prayer. Most of all, she loved the meaning behind the praying hands, which she and Claudine had often talked about. The words that her mother frequently spoke came to her mind: "When in doubt, pray it out." Along with the necklace was a moist paper towel holding a small bundle of freshly picked forget-me-nots.

Jewel and Claudine started right back where they left off. Except for days when the weather was bad, not a day went by when there wasn't a letter waiting to be read in the mailbox by the creek.

EPILOGUE

The summer days slowly began to turn cooler with autumn just around the corner. At the end of the long, dusty dirt road, a giant squeaking school bus came to a halt to pick up two little girls.

Seated side by side, their knees propped on the seat in front of them, Jewel and Claudine rode the bumpy bus over the hills and through the winding roads to a small school just over the way. Giggling the whole way there and again on their way back at the end of the school day, they had not a care in the world.

After hopping off the bus, they walked back down the long dirt road. As they reached Claudine's house, the two friends hugged and once again shared a pinkie promise to meet at their usual spot after homework and supper. Jewel looked down and saw a single blue flower not yet taken by the first frost. She reached down and picked it, handing it to her friend. "Same spot?"

"For sure!" Claudine shouted as she trotted up her long driveway. When she was halfway to her house, she turned back and cupped her hands over her mouth. "See you in a little while at the mailbox by the creek!"

BEHIND THE STORY

(Top) Side view of Claudine's house with Jewel's house on the other side of the creek in the distance; (bottom) Blackburn Hollow Road leading to Jewel and Claudine's house at the end of the road.

*P*oliomyelitis, a contagious viral infection that attacks the central nervous system and often leaves its victims partially or fully paralyzed, infected tens of thousands of Americans throughout the 1940s and 1950s. Polio epidemics occurred, especially in the summer months. Like clockwork, each June in America, newspapers, including the *Wilkes Journal Patriot*, a newspaper printed in North Wilkesboro, North Carolina, began reporting about new polio cases. Children were warned not to jump into puddles or share food with friends. Most swimming pools closed, and if movie theatres remained open, they warned people not to sit too close to one another.

Although polio wasn't limited to children, they seemed to be the most at risk for contracting the horrible virus. Polio, also known as infantile paralysis, crippled hundreds of children in North Carolina, hitting particularly hard during the 1940s. The mountain communities didn't have good medical facilities, so they would often send the sick to nearby hospitals, such as Statesville.

Because of the polio epidemic in and around these hospitals, they became overcrowded. In an effort to treat more patients, particularly infants and children, an emergency hospital was set up in Hickory, North Carolina. This hospital, known formally as the Emergency Infantile Paralysis Hospital, was referred to as "The Miracle of Hickory."

As the disease continued spreading, many communities in NC encouraged parents to keep their children inside during the summer months or at least limit their activity to things close to their house and away from other children. This quarantine affected real-life friends Jewel and Claudine. They came up with a makeshift mailbox by the creek to communicate with each other until they were able to reunite again.

Jewel (left) with her uncle Bruce and sister Martha in front of creek and Claudine's house

Although it was not uncommon to hear about an infant or a young child in the community catching it, thankfully, polio, nor anything resembling it, did not actually strike in Jewel or Claudine's homes. Even so, their parents continued to caution their children to keep their distance during that particularly dreadful summer epidemic.

Finally, in 1955, a successful polio vaccine was made available to the United States by Dr. Jonas Salk. In 1959, North Carolina became the first state to require that all children get the polio vaccine.

Although Jewel later moved to Winston-Salem and Claudine remained in Wilkes County, the girls kept in touch through special events, cards, and letters. In their elderly years, the two friends reunited one last time when Claudine attended Jewel's sixty-fifth wedding anniversary. Even though Jewel and Claudine didn't see each other as often as they would have liked, they were true to their promise and remained friends forever. Both died at age 87, Claudine in the fall of 2018, and Jewel in the spring of 2019.

Ironically, in the spring of 2020, one year after my mother, Jewel, passed away, I experienced a pandemic referred to as COVID-19. Because of a shelter-in-place order to try and slow down the spread of this virus, my life as a schoolteacher changed drastically. Schools closed their doors, and I had to continue teaching my second-grade students through videos, online resources, and other creative ways. Although this pandemic caused fear and altered many things about a "normal life," it also brought some positive things. I was able to catch a glimpse of what life must have been like for my mother many years ago. Time seemed to slow down, enabling me to complete this book based on the true events that my mother often told me on our visits to the site of her family's home in Purlear,

(Above left) Jewel at age 12; (top right) Claudine's house, present day; (center) Jewel's house, present day; (bottom) Side view of Jewel's house showing the attic where she wanted a bedroom

just outside of North Wilkesboro, North Carolina. During our visits, as we crossed over the creek on the long, dusty dirt road in the hills of Blackburn's Hollow, Mama would tell me about the summer of the polio epidemic that kept her from her playmate. It was the summer that altered her normal life, forcing her to use creativity to communicate with her friend, thus creating a makeshift mailbox to mail her "Letters by the Creek."

(Above left): the shed behind Jewel's house; (center): The Creek running through Blackburn's Hollow; (bottom): Jim's garage.

ACKNOWLEDGMENTS

I would like to thank the following for their valuable help in making this book possible.

Most importantly, I thank my Lord and Savior for blessing me with wonderful Christian parents who shared their memories with us. I thank Him for the gift of being able to put the memories shared into words, forming my first book. Just like He did in this story, I thank Him for being my Healer, my Refuge, and my Strength.

My precious Mama for being a great storyteller and knowing the value of sharing the memories of her childhood with her children and grandchildren. Mama was quite the storyteller. She taught me well in that when telling a story, if you can't remember it all, just make up the rest!

My sweet Aunt Carol for filling in the gaps and sharing her memories when my mother was no longer around to ask while I was completing this book.

My husband, Greg, my children, Jessica, Jordan, Josh, and granddaughter Braelynn, who gave me a break while I worked on the book. Jessica read the book several times, and Jordan rode with me to Blackburn's Hollow to take pictures of the setting.

My brothers Randy and Steve and sister-in-laws Lori

and Vikki, for keeping Mama and Daddy's stories alive as well as preserving the photos. It is truly a blessing to be able to share these with our own children.

My friend and illustrator, Justin, who brought the photographs and images to life through creative and wonderful illustrations.

My sister-in-law, Kim, for reading a draft of the book and offering suggestions.

Midge, Claudine's baby sister, for allowing me to use her name and character in the book.

Randy and Kim, the present owners of my mother's homeplace, for always making my family feel welcome when we go to visit and allowing us to walk around on their property to take the photos.

The present owners of Claudine's homeplace for allowing me to take and use photos of their house.

To my friends and family that gave me encouragement along the way to complete the book.

References

Polio: The Iron Lung and Other Equipment
https://amhistory.si.edu/polio/howpolio/ironlung.htm

The Miracle of Hickory
https://www.ourstate.com/the-miracle-of-hickory/

What is Polio?
https://www.cdc.gov/polio/what-is-polio/index.
htm?CDC_AA_refVal=https%3A%2F%2Fwww.cdc.
gov%2Fpolio%2Fabout%2Findex.htm

Recalling Viruses Past: House Calls, Quarantine Signs
https://eastgreenwichnews.com/recalling-viruses-past-
house-calls-quarantine-signs/

Wilkes Journal-Patriot: Polio epidemic was scary time
https://www.journalpatriot.com/opinion/polio-epidem-
ic-was-scary-time/article_33c46a6e-89a0-11ea-a4b4-
8b75db59a3a8.html

Meet the Author

Julie Hart is a Christian, wife, mother and Mimi as well as a second grade school-teacher with a love for sharing personal and inspirational experiences. She loves retelling stories that were told to her as a child. One of her favorite memories growing up was sitting around the dinner table with her parents and two brothers telling stories. She said, "We never grew tired of the funny ones as well as the stories my parents told of how things were when they were young." If there's one piece of advice she could give to her children and students, it is this: "Always listen when someone tells you a story because it just might turn into a book one day."

Meet the Illustrator

Justin Branch loves telling stories too! Whether it's by drawing pictures, taking photos, writing songs and making music, he loves using his imagination to help bring stories to life. He is a follower of Jesus, husband, father to two amazing kids and a longtime pal of the author!